P9-DNQ-404

THE LAST LEAF

*This American classic
is presented without adaptation as part
of the Creative Classic series.*

Other Stories by O. Henry

THE LAST
LEAF
BY O. HENRY

Illustrated by Byron Glaser

Holgate Branch Library
Holgate, Ohio
81-696

Creative Education, Inc.
Mankato, Minnesota

Book Design: Neumeier Design Team

Published by Creative Education, Inc.
123 South Broad Street, Mankato, Minnesota 56001

Copyright © 1980 by Creative Education, Inc. International copyrights reserved in all countries.
No part of this book may be reproduced in any form without written permission from the publisher.
Printed in the United States.

Library of Congress Cataloging in Publication Data

Porter, William Sydney, 1862-1910.
    The last leaf.

    SUMMARY: A sick artist with no will to live feels she will die when the last leaf falls from the
tree by her window—yet for some reason the leaf hangs on.
    [1. Artists—Fiction. 2. Death—Fiction] I. Title.
PZ7.P834Las 1980   [Fic]   80-21651
ISBN 0-87191-774-2

To
the continuation of fine literature
for readers of all ages.

THE LAST
LEAF
BY O. HENRY

west of Washington Square the streets have run crazy and broken themselves into small strips called "places." These "places" make strange angles and curves. One Street crosses itself a time or two. An artist once discovered a valuable possibility in this street. Suppose a collector with a bill for paints, paper and canvas should, in traversing this route, suddenly meet himself coming back, without a cent having been paid on account!

So, to quaint old Greenwich Village the art people soon came prowling, hunting for north windows and eighteenth-century gables and Dutch attics and low rents. Then they imported some pewter mugs and a chafing dish or two from Sixth Avenue, and became a "colony."

At the top of a squatty, three-story brick Sue and Johnsy had their studio. "Johnsy" was familiar for Joanna. One was from Maine; the other from California. They had met at the *table d'hôte* of an Eighth Street "Delmonico's," and found their tastes in art, chicory salad and bishop sleeves so congenial that the joint studio resulted.

That was in May. In November a cold, unseen stranger, whom the doctors called Pneumonia, stalked about the colony, touching one here and there with his icy fingers. Over on the east side this ravager strode boldly, smiting his victims by scores, but his feet trod slowly through the maze of the narrow and moss-grown "places."

Mr. Pneumonia was not what you would call a chivalric old gentleman. A mite of a little woman with blood thinned by California zephyrs was hardly fair game for the red-fisted, short-breathed old duffer. But Johnsy he smote; and she lay, scarcely moving, on her painted iron bedstead, looking through the small Dutch window-panes at the blank side of the next brick house.

One morning the busy doctor invited Sue into the hallway with a shaggy, gray eyebrow.

"She has one chance in — let us say, ten," he said, as he shook down the mercury in his clinical thermometer. "And that chance is for her to want to live. This way people have of lining-up on the side of the undertaker makes the entire pharmacopoeia look silly. Your little lady has made up her mind that she's not going to get well. Has she anything on her mind?"

"She — she wanted to paint the Bay of Naples some day." said Sue.

"Paint? — bosh! Has she anything on her mind worth thinking about twice — a man for instance?"

"A man?" said Sue, with a jew's-harp twang in her voice. "Is a man worth — but, no, doctor; there is nothing of the kind."

"Well, it is the weakness, then," said the doctor. "I will do all that science, so far as it may filter through my efforts, can accomplish. But whenever my patient begins to count the carriages in her funeral procession I subtract 50 per cent from the curative power of medicines. If you will get her to ask one question about the new winter styles in cloak sleeves I will promise you a one-in-five chance for her, instead of one in ten."

After the doctor had gone Sue went into the workroom and cried a Japanese napkin to a pulp. Then she swaggered into Johnsy's room with her drawing board, whistling ragtime.

Johnsy lay, scarcely making a ripple under the bedclothes, with her face toward the window. Sue stopped whistling, thinking she was asleep.

She arranged her board and began a pen-and-ink drawing to illustrate a magazine story. Young artists must pave their way to Art by drawing pictures for magazine stories that young authors write to pave their way to Literature.

As Sue was sketching a pair of elegant horseshow riding trousers and a monocle of the figure of the hero, an Idaho cowboy, she heard a low sound, several times repeated. She went quickly to the bedside.

Johnsy's eyes were open wide. She was looking out the window and counting — counting backward.

Johnsy's eyes were open wide. She was looking out the window and counting — counting backward.

"Twelve," she said, and little later "eleven"; and then "ten," and "nine"; and then "eight" and "seven", almost together.

Sue looked solicitously out of the window. What was there to count? There was only a bare, dreary yard to be seen, and the blank side of the brick house twenty feet away. An old, old ivy vine, gnarled and decayed at the roots, climbed half way up the brick wall. The cold breath of autumn had stricken its leaves from the vine until its skeleton branches clung, almost bare, to the crumbling bricks.

"What is it, dear?" asked Sue.

"Six," said Johnsy, in almost a whisper. "They're falling faster now. Three days ago there were almost a hundred. It made my head ache to count them. But now it's easy. There goes another one. There are only five left now."

"Five what, dear? Tell your Sudie."

"Leaves. On the ivy vine. When the last one falls I must go, too. I've known that for three days. Didn't the doctor tell you?"

"Oh, I never heard of such nonsense," complained Sue, with magnificent scorn. "What have old ivy leaves to do with your getting well? And you used to love that vine so, you naughty girl. Don't be a goosey. Why, the doctor told me this morning that your chances for getting well real soon were — let's see exactly what he said — he said the chances were ten to one! Why, that's almost as good a chance as we have in New York when we ride on the street cars or walk past a new building. Try to take some broth now, and let Sudie go back to her drawing, so she can sell the editor man with it, and buy port wine for her sick child, and pork chops for her greedy self."

"You needn't get any more wine," said Johnsy, keeping her eyes fixed out the window. "There goes another. No, I don't want any broth. That leaves just four. I want to see the last one fall before it gets dark. Then I'll go, too."

"Johnsy, dear," said Sue, bending over her, "will you promise me to keep your eyes closed, and not look out the window until I am done working? I must hand those drawings in by to-morrow. I need the light, or I would draw the shade down."

"Couldn't you draw in the other room?" asked Johnsy, coldly.

"I'd rather be here by you," said Sue. "Beside, I don't want you to keep looking at those silly ivy leaves."

"Tell me as soon as you have finished," said Johnsy, closing her eyes, and lying white and still as a fallen statue, "because I want to see the last one fall. I'm tired of waiting. I'm tired of thinking. I want to turn loose my hold on everything, and go sailing down, down, just like one of those poor, tired leaves."

"Try to sleep," said Sue. "I must call Behrman up to be my model for the old hermit miner. I'll not be gone a minute. Don't try to move 'til I come back."

Old Behrman was a painter who lived on the ground floor beneath them. He was past sixty and had a Michael Angelo's Moses beard curling down from the head of a satyr along the body of an imp. Behrman was a failure in art. Forty years he had wielded the brush without getting near enough to touch the hem of his Mistress's robe. He had been always about to paint a masterpiece, but had never yet begun it. For several years he had painted nothing except now and then a daub in the line of commerce or advertising. He earned a little by serving as a model to those young artists in the colony who could not pay the price of a professional. He drank gin to excess, and still talked of his coming masterpiece. For the rest he was a fierce little old man, who scoffed terribly at softness in any one, and who regarded himself as especial mastiff-in-waiting to protect the two young artists in the studio above.

Sue found Behrman smelling strongly of juniper berries in his dimly lighted den below. In one corner was a blank canvas on an easel that had been waiting there for twenty-five years to receive the first line of the masterpiece. She told him of Johnsy's fancy, and how she feared she would, indeed, light and fragile as a leaf herself, float away, when her slight hold upon the world grew weaker.

Old Behrman, with his red eyes plainly streaming, shouted his contempt and derision for such idiotic imaginings.

"Vass!" he cried. "Is dere people in de world mit der foolishness to die because leafs dey drop off from a confounded vine? I haf not heard of such a thing. No, I will not bose as a model for your fool hermit-dunderhead. Vy do you allow dot silly pusiness to come in der brain of her? Ach, dot poor leetle Miss Yohnsy."

"She is very ill and weak," said Sue, "and the fever has left her mind morbid and full of strange fancies. Very well, Mr. Behrman, if you do not care to pose for me, you needn't. But I think you are a horrid old — old flibbertigibbet."

"You are just like a woman!" yelled Behrman. "Who said I will not bose? Go on. I come mit you. For half an hour I haf peen trying to say dot I am ready to bose. Gott! dis is not any blace in which one so goot as Miss Yohnsy shall lie sick. Some day I vill baint a masterpiece, and ve shall all go away. Gott! yes."

Johnsy was sleeping when they went upstairs. Sue pulled the shade down to the window-sill, and motioned Behrman into the other room. In there they peered out the window fearfully at the ivy vine.

Then they looked at each other for a moment without speaking. A persistent, cold rain was falling, mingled with snow. Behrman, in his old blue shirt, took his seat as the hermit miner on an upturned kettle for a rock.

When Sue awoke from an hour's sleep the next morning she found Johnsy with dull, wide-open eyes staring at the drawn green shade.

"Pull it up; I want to see," she ordered, in a whisper.

Wearily Sue obeyed.

But, lo! after the beating rain and fierce gusts of wind that had endured through the livelong night, there yet stood out against the brick wall one ivy leaf. It was the last one on the vine. Still dark green near its stem, with its serrated edges tinted with the yellow of dissolution and decay, it hung bravely from a branch some twenty feet above the ground.

"It is the last one," said Johnsy. "I thought it would surely fall during the night. I heard the wind. It will fall to-day, and I shall die at the same time."

"Dear, dear!" said Sue, leaning her worn face down to the pillow, "think of me, if you won't think of yourself. What would I do?"

But Johnsy did not answer. The lonesomest thing in all the world is a soul when it is making ready to go on its mysterious, far journey. The fancy seemed to possess her more strongly as one by one the ties that bound her to friendship and to earth were loosed.

The day wore away, and even through the twilight they could see the lone ivy leaf clinging to its stem against the wall. And then, with the coming of the night the north wind was again loosed, while the rain still beat against the windows and pattered down from the low Dutch eaves.

When it was light enough Johnsy, the merciless, commanded that the shade be raised.

The ivy leaf was still there.

Johnsy lay for a long time looking at it. And then she called to Sue, who was stirring her chicken broth over the gas stove.

"I've been a bad girl, Sudie," said Johnsy. "Something has made that last leaf stay there to show me how wicked I was. It is a sin to want to die. You may bring me a little broth now, and some milk with a

"Even chances," said the doctor, taking Sue's thin, shaking hand in
his. "With good nursing you'll win."

Holgate Branch Library
Holgate, Ohio

little port in it, and—no; bring me a hand-mirror first, and then pack some pillows about me, and I will sit up and watch you cook."

An hour later she said:

"Sudie, some day I hope to paint the Bay of Naples."

The doctor came in the afternoon, and Sue had an excuse to go into the hallway as he left.

"Even chances," said the doctor, taking Sue's thin, shaking hand in his. "With good nursing you'll win. And now I must see another case I have downstairs. Behrman, his name is—some kind of an artist, I believe. Pneumonia, too. He is an old, weak man, and the attack is acute. There is no hope for him; but he goes to the hospital to-day to be made more comfortable."

The next day the doctor said to Sue: "She's out of danger. You've won. Nutrition and care now—that's all."

And that afternoon Sue came to the bed where Johnsy lay, contentedly knitting a very blue and very useless woollen shoulder scarf, and put one arm around her, pillows and all.

"I have something to tell you, white mouse," she said. "Mr. Behrman died of pneumonia to-day in the hospital. He was ill only two days. The janitor found him in the morning of the first day in his room downstairs helpless with pain. His shoes and clothing were wet through and icy cold. They couldn't imagine where he had been on such a dreadful night. And then they found a lantern, still lighted, and a ladder that had been dragged from its place, and some scattered brushes, and a palette with green and yellow colors mixed on it, and — look out the window, dear, at the last ivy leaf on the wall. Didn't you wonder why it never fluttered or moved when the wind blew? Ah, darling, it's Behrman's masterpiece — he painted it there the night that the last leaf fell."

O. Henry
1862-1910

O HENRY, a man with many names, knew how to tell a story. He was born William Sidney Porter on September 11, 1862, and he died Will S. Parker on June 5, 1910. In between, he was best known as O. Henry, an important American short story writer. During his lifetime, William had almost as many careers and experiences as he had stories to tell.

William was born to Algernon Sidney Porter and Mary Jane Virginia Swaim in Greensboro, North Carolina. His father, a physician by profession, preferred to spend his time working out mechanical inventions. His mother was a well-educated and enterprising woman, but she died when William was only three. He was then brought up by his aunt.

William attended school where his aunt was teacher. But school wasn't very important in those days, because nearly everyone was involved in the Reconstruction after the Civil War. So William left school at 15 and went to work in his uncle's drugstore. Apparently, people thought of William as bright, cheerful, talented, especially in drawing, and an avid reader.

At 19, William traveled to Texas to seek his fortune.

He lived on a ranch, learning the ways of cowboys. Later, he wrote many stories about the cowboys in the West. He tried writing a few stories during this period, but he wasn't very good at it yet.

Two years later he moved on to Austin where the University of Texas offered him many opportunities to make stimulating friendships. From his friends and acquaintances, William constantly picked up story ideas.

In Austin, William was first a bookkeeper, then a draftsman, and then a bank teller. He fell in love with Athol Estes and they eloped in 1887. To supplement his salary at the bank, William started sending his anecdotes to various newspapers. By 1894, William felt he could quit his job at the bank and spend all his time writing for newspapers. A publisher in Houston read some of his stories and offered him a job.

Just about that time, the bank accused him of having stolen some money. While his guilt was questionable, William panicked and fled to New Orleans. Then he sailed out of the country to Honduras.

He hid there until early in 1897 when he heard that his wife was seriously ill. He returned; yet despite his tender nursing, she died later that year. Early in 1898, William was sentenced to a 5-year term in the Ohio Penitentiary for a crime he felt he didn't commit.

Being a registered pharmacist, William had a rather easy job in the drugstore in prison. Yet he keenly felt the disgrace of being in prison. He saw only a few of the other prisoners — and those were men whose stories of the West interested him. William wrote a great deal in prison — it was his way of dealing with the sadness in his life. He published many stories during this time, and all under assumed names. O. Henry was the one that stuck.

After leaving prison, William went to New York. He spent about a year just walking the streets and parks, observing the experiences and expressions of men and women. There, in New York, William felt he had found himself. Slowly, he developed the kind of story for which he became famous.

His stories almost always rely on irony and unexpected outcomes. For instance, in the story, "The Gift of the Magi," the husband sells his watch to buy combs for his wife's hair, and his wife sells her hair to buy a chain for his watch. All William's characters are simple and familiar. The twists of fate turn up in all his stories but not in bitter ways. And his plain language, dotted with slang, makes it all the easier for readers to identify with the characters and the consequences.

While William lived in New York, his stories were in constant demand. He wrote 65 stories in 1904; 50 stories in 1905; and he gathered up many of his stories in semi-annual books. *The Four Million* and *The Trimmed Lamp* were the most well known.

Though William was surrounded by people in New York, he ached with loneliness. In 1907, he married Sara Coleman, a friend from Greensboro. But within a few years they were living separately. It was really only when this great story teller died in 1910 that his stories became famous worldwide. And since then, nearly everyone who likes a good story has a couple of O. Henry's to tell.

jf   81-696

Henry, O

    T

jf   81-696

        Henry, O
AUTHOR
        The Last Leaf.
TITLE

DATE DUE	BORROWER'S NAME
AUG 20 '9	J. Perk
MY 15 '01	Aubrey Knick

DA

A

M

**Holgate Community Branch
Library**
136 Wilhelm St.
Holgate, Ohio 43527

DEMCO